Doggie Dreams

by Nancy Kapp Chapman

illustrated by Lee Chapman

G. P. Putnam's Sons

New York

Some dogs dream of bones and such,

A cozy home,

A gentle touch.

Some dogs dream of chasing cats,

Three meals a day,

Or catching rats!

But some dogs dream as people do—

Hard to believe, and yet it's true!

These dogs dream of earning big bones

With a job,

an office,

and cellular phones!

These doggies dream of their own place to eat
Where people can't come in—
they stay in the street!

These doggies dream of going to **school**
Where **barking** and **howling** is the rule.

Here's a dog with a wonderful goal:
She dreams of digging the

largest hole!

This dog dreams of being

the best,

With lots of medals

on his chest!

This dog dreams of making the rounds
Driving a bus that's loaded with hounds.

Pilot-Pooch dreams of flying a plane—
High in the sky through the wind and the rain.

This dog is riding **tall** in the saddle

Dreaming of rounding up all the cattle.

To fly through the air
with grace and ease,
These daring dogs dream
of the circus trapeze!

With two paws up
and two on the
ground,
These dogs dream
of applause
all around!

There is no limit to this
dog's ambition,
Reading the news on
the *Morning Edition.*

These dogs dream

of being cool

Rock-and-rolling

after school!

Here is one very strange Dalmatian

Who has a dream of leading the nation.

These dogs dream of planets and

stars.

Do you suppose there are dogs on

Mars?

So now you know

that when dogs dream

It's not always

what it may seem.

For in their dreams

they just may be

Very much like you and me...

For all the dogs everywhere

G. P. Putnam's Sons
a division of Penguin Putnam Books for Young Readers, 345 Hudson Street, New York, NY 10014.
G. P. Putnam's Sons, Reg. U.S. Pat. & Tm. Off. Published simultaneously in Canada.
Printed in Hong Kong by South China Printing Co. (1988) Ltd.
Designed by Semadar Megged. Text set in Engine.
The art for this book was done in oil paint on canvas with the occasional dog hair mixed in.
Library of Congress Cataloging-in-Publication Data
Chapman, Nancy Kapp. Doggie dreams / Nancy Kapp Chapman; illustrated by Lee Chapman. p. cm.
Summary: Some dogs have simple dreams of bones or chasing cats, while others envision grander things,
such as flying a plane or even being president.
[1. Dogs—Fiction. 2. Dreams—Fiction. 3. Stories in rhyme.]
I. Chapman, Lee, ill. II. Title PZ8.3.C373Do 2000 [E]—dc21 99-27373 CIP
ISBN 0-399-23443-8
1 3 5 7 9 10 8 6 4 2
First Impression